DATE			

Stranger in the Mirror

ALLEN SAY

Houghton Mifflin Company
Boston   1995

To Walter and Kathleen

Walter Lorraine ⟨wk⟩ Books

Copyright © 1995 by Allen Say

All rights reserved. For information about permission to
reproduce selections from this book, write to Permissions,
Houghton Mifflin Company, 215 Park Avenue South,
New York, New York 10003.

Library of Congress Cataloging-in-Publication Data

Say, Allen.
   Stranger in the mirror / by Allen Say.
      p.   cm.
   Summary: When a young Asian-American boy who spends all of his
time skateboarding wakes up one morning with the face of an old man,
he has trouble convincing people that he is still himself.
   ISBN 0-395-61590-9
   [1. Old age—Fiction.   2. Skateboarding—Fiction.   3. Asian
Americans—Fiction.]   I. Title.
PZ7.S2744St   1995   95-2296
[E]—dc20   CIP   R01132 46959
                            AC

Printed in the United States of America

HOR   10   9   8   7   6   5   4   3   2   1

Stranger in the Mirror

Sam came home late.

He opened the front door and hesitated.

The house seemed strange and empty now. Sam missed
hearing the raspy voice and the shuffling of slippers.

He couldn't forget how small Grandpa had looked
waving good-bye.

"I don't want to get old," he thought.

Next morning, Sam woke up feeling tired. When he
went downstairs his family was already in the kitchen.
He started to say good morning when a great commotion
broke out. Chairs crashed. Dishes shattered.
"What's wrong?" Sam asked.
"Why are you looking at me like that?"
They only stared. Sam turned and looked in
the hallway mirror.

A stranger with white hair and a wrinkled face
looked back at him. He rubbed his eyes. The stranger
did the same. Sam was looking at himself!
"Grandpa!" Jessie cried.
Covering his face, Sam ran up to his room and
slammed the door.
When Mother and Father called to him, Sam cried,
"Go away! I don't want to see anybody!"
He buried his face in a pillow.
"Son, we have to get you to the doctor," Father said.
"He will know what's wrong."

In the doctor's waiting room, Sam whispered to his mother,
"What's going to happen to me? What's the doctor
going to do to me?"
"Everything will be fine, Sam," Mother answered.
"He'll examine you and decide what to do."
"You're not going to send me away, are you?"
"What do you mean? What are you saying?"
"You know, where Grandpa went."
"Sam, you're only a boy. What a question!"

Dr. Chang didn't recognize Sam. But when he saw
the birthmark on his back, he called his partner,
Dr. Bloom. The two doctors took turns examining
Sam from head to toe.

"Idiopathic dermal development," Dr. Chang announced.

"What do you mean?" Sam's mother demanded.

"Some sort of skin condition," Dr. Bloom explained.
"Everything else seems to be in order."

"Can't you do *anything?*" Sam's mother asked.

"I think wait and see would be the prudent course
for now," Dr. Bloom replied.

"What about school?"

"I see no reason why he cannot attend school,"
Dr. Chang said.

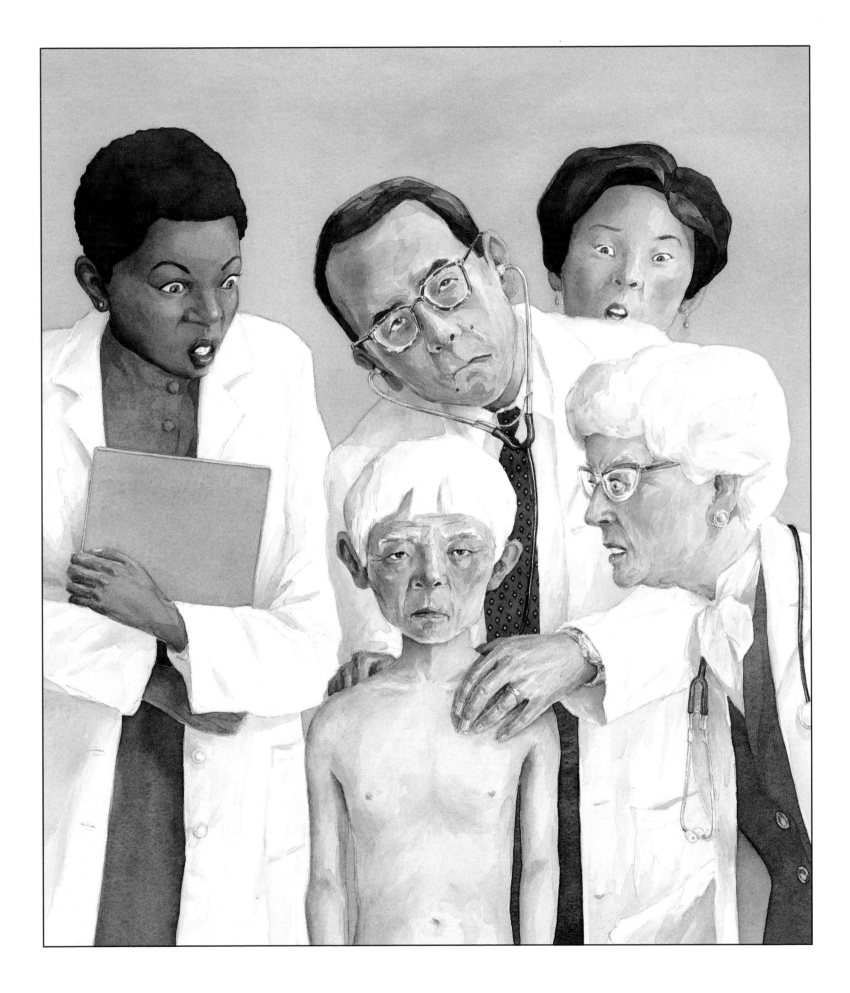

So Sam went to school.

"Well, what do we have here?" his teacher said.

"I'm Sam, Ms. Hench," he said. "I sit over there, next to Melissa."

"Cool mask, Sam!" Josh yelled from the back.

"Not so fast, little man," Ms. Hench stood in his way.

"How do I know you're really Sam?"

"You sent me to the principal's office, Ms. Hench. I slid the rail on my skateboard, don't you remember?"

Ms. Hench dropped her book and sat on her desk.

"Take your seat until I can find out about this," she said.

"That's not a mask!" Melissa announced.

"His wrinkles are all wiggly!"

"Look, he's really old!" someone shouted.

"Rip Van . . . Wrinkle!" Josh laughed.

Sam hid his face in a book.

At recess, the whole school came out to look at Sam.

"Are you really Sam?" they asked. He nodded.

"What happened?"

"You must have done something bad. Smoking, I bet."

"No, I didn't! Leave me alone!" Sam yelled.

"He sounds just like old Sam, ha ha!"

They followed him everywhere. Even the teachers
stopped and stared.

"I thought Josh was my friend . . ." Sam said
under his breath.

After school, he covered his head with the hood
on his jacket and ran home.

At dinner, no one said a word.

When Jessie was ready for bed, she came to Sam's room.

"Are you going to move downstairs?" she asked.

"No. Why?" Sam sat up.

"Just wondered," she said. "Grandpa's room's down there."

"What are you saying, Jessie?" he started to get up
but she was gone.

Sam couldn't sleep. He got up to go to the bathroom
and saw a light in the kitchen. Then he heard
his parents whispering.

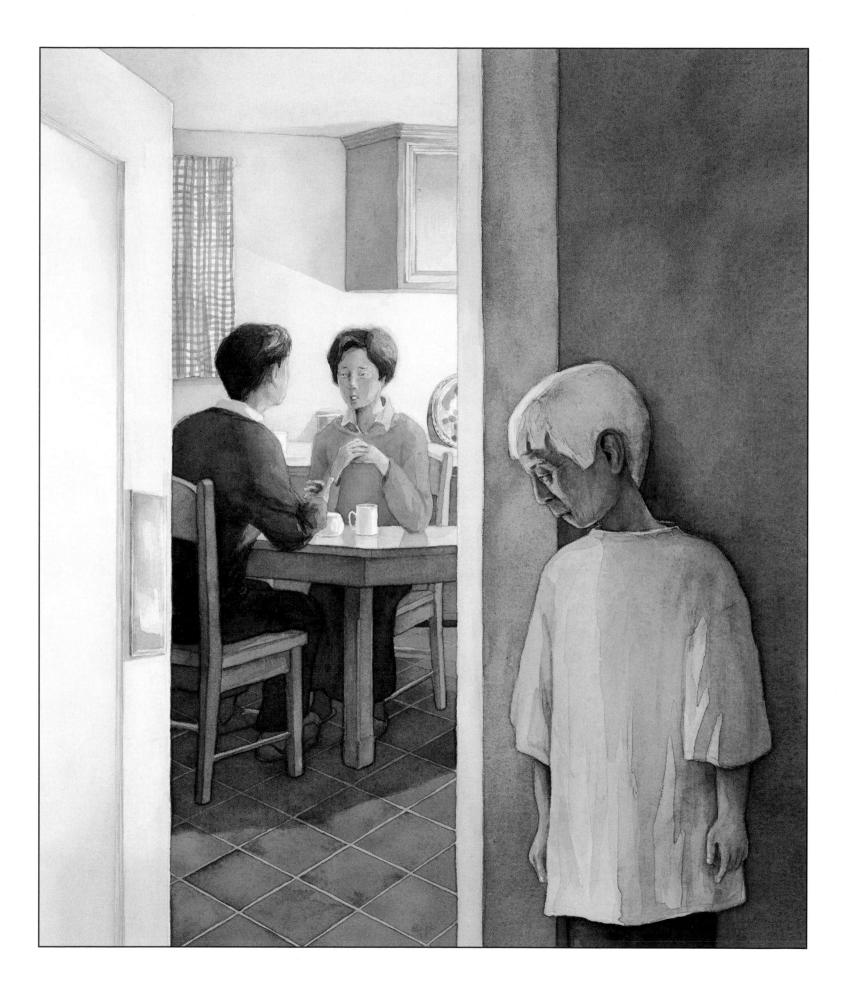

Next day at school, the teasing continued. Sam remained at his desk and didn't say a word to anyone until the final bell. Then he ran home.

The house was empty. Quickly he made three salami sandwiches in the kitchen and took them to his room. He packed some clothes in his backpack and put the sandwiches on top. He then took all his money out of a jar, picked up the bag, and went downstairs.

He was just sneaking out the back door when he heard a crash in the alleyway. He looked up and saw something tumbling through the air. It looked like a model airplane with no wings. It was a skateboard.

"Hey!" Sam cried.

Without thinking, he dropped his bag and hopped onto the skateboard. Suddenly the whole world rattled and vibrated. The wind and speed made him breathe fast. All his worries flew from his mind. He forgot he wasn't going home anymore. He forgot he was old.

"Give me back my deck!" someone shouted after him. Sam didn't hear. He was laughing.

Only moments later Sam was coasting through
the playground at his school. He kick-flipped and
heel-flipped. He did nose-slides and tail-slides.
"Look at the old man go!" someone shouted.
"That's Sam, the kid in Ms. Hench's class!"
"He does rail-slides!"
They started to clap their hands. Then they cheered,
shouting encouragements. Sam didn't seem to hear
or see them. He went on skating.

"Hey, that's my skateboard!" A boy came panting
from the gate. Sam hopped off, nodded, and walked away.
When he reached the street, he stopped suddenly and
cried aloud, "My bag!" He broke into a run.
The backpack was gone. He sat down on the steps.
"Looking for something?" a small voice said.
He looked up and saw Jessie peeking out the window.
"What did you do with it?" Sam asked in a loud voice.
"You don't have to be rude. It's in your room," Jessie said.
"Did you open it?"
"No, I didn't. And you're welcome."
"Thank you, thank you!" Sam shouted and ran up to his room.
It wasn't there.
He rushed downstairs and burst into Grandpa's old room.
The bag was on the bed. Shaking his head,
Sam carried it upstairs.

"She really thinks I'm Grandpa," Sam sighed. "Nobody
knows me anymore. Melissa and Josh won't talk to me now.
Even Mom and Dad think I'm somebody else.
Where can I go?"
He ate a sandwich, and as he looked around the room, he
noticed his skateboard.
"That was fun," he said, remembering. "Pretty good
for an old man. But what's the difference? Who cares what
I look like? I'm Sam. Nobody can change that."
Suddenly he felt very tired. He lay down and
instantly fell asleep.

Sam didn't wake up until early the next morning.
He quickly put on his shoes, picked up his bag, and
tiptoed down the stairs. He was nearly out
of the house when he felt as if someone were
watching him. He jerked his head around and saw a
stranger in the hallway mirror. He had shiny black hair
and a smooth face. Sam rubbed his eyes. The stranger
did the same. Sam shrieked.
Mother and Father and Jessie came running from their rooms.
"What are you doing?" they shouted at once.
"I'm Sam! I'm a boy again!" he cried.
"You scared us half to death!" Father said.
"Do you know what time it is?"
"I thought the house was on fire!" Mother said.
Shaking their heads, they returned to their room.
"Why aren't they getting up? We have to go to
school," Sam said.
"It's Sunday, silly," Jessie told him.

Sam walked outside and Jessie followed.

He opened the backpack, nearly tearing off the straps.

He stared inside—at the two squashed sandwiches.

"So that's what you had in there!" Jessie exclaimed.

"Did you put my bag in Grandpa's room yesterday?" he asked.

Jessie looked at him. 'Why did you get up so early?" she asked.

"Well, I thought . . . it was Monday. Want a sandwich?"

"Sure, if it isn't tuna fish."

And so they ate the sandwiches.